BARK AT THE PARK

LEILA & NUGGET MYSTERY #3

Allison! Have fun
with Leila + Nugget.

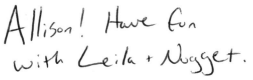

DESERAE & DUSTIN BRADY

CONTENTS

OTHER BOOKS BY DUSTIN BRADY

Superhero for a Day: The Magic Magic Eight Ball

Trapped in a Video Game: Book One
Trapped in a Video Game: Book Two
Trapped in a Video Game: Book Three
Trapped in a Video Game: Book Four

Who Stole Mr. T? Leila & Nugget Mystery #1
The Case With No Clues: Leila & Nugget
Mystery #2

ACKNOWLEDGMENTS

Special thanks to April Brady for the cover and interior illustrations. You can follow April's artwork on Instagram: @aprilynnart.

BIG DOG

"Excuse me! Sorry. Whoops! Nugget, slow down!" Third-grader Leila Beal struggled to pull back her little dog, Nugget, as he sprinted ahead.

"Just let the little guy enjoy himself," Leila's friend, Kait, said.

"I would, but he's tangling everyone up in his leash!"

Nugget couldn't help it. He'd never

seen so many new friends in his life. Leila and Kait had joined over 200 people and their dogs, all decked out in Middleburg Red Dogs gear, inside their town's minor league baseball stadium. Today was the Red Dogs' eighth annual "Bark at the Park" game, where fans were allowed to bring their dogs to the ballpark. While the special day had started as a fun, little promotion, it'd quickly grown to become one of the town's biggest traditions. The coolest part of Bark at the Park was always the Pup Parade around the bases to start the game. Then there were special treats and activities for the dogs throughout the afternoon. Finally, after the baseball game was over, the Middleburg Dog of the Year would be crowned.

This was Leila's first-ever Bark at the Park, and she couldn't have been more excited about it. To celebrate, she'd even made Nugget his own Red Dogs hat with a little strap. Of course, he wasn't wearing it now because he'd freaked out once she'd put it on his head, but Leila still brought it to the game just in case. She'd also convinced Kait to bring her grandparents' old Scottish Terrier, Baxter. Baxter was not amused.

"It's OK, Bax," Kait said to the grumbling, little dog. "We're gonna do the parade soon, then we can eat snacks for the rest of the afternoon!"

As if on cue, a woman in a suit walked on top of the dugout and tried to get all of the dog owners' attention. "Thank you for coming, everyone!" she yelled over the barking. She waited until the dogs quieted down to continue. "This might be our biggest Bark at the Park yet! I'm going to ask you all to follow me

3

underneath the stadium. We'll be a little cramped for a second, but don't worry—Big Dog will be right there to lead us onto the field for the Pup Parade. OK, let's go!" The woman climbed back down and unlocked a door next to the dugout.

Leila, Kait and their dogs followed the crowd through the door. They walked down a few stairs and entered an old hallway that smelled like moldy laundry. The woman was right—it was super cramped. This hallway was made for players to get to the clubhouse, not 200 dogs to squish into.

Baxter started whining. Kait picked him up. "I know, little buddy. I don't like crowds either." She turned to Leila. "What are we waiting for? Some big dog?"

"No, not a big dog. Big Dog. The mascot."

Kait wrinkled her nose. "A big, red dog? You mean Clifford?"

"No. It's just 'Big Dog.' Also, they don't like people calling him 'Clifford.' I think they might have gotten sued once."

Kait still looked confused.

"Haven't you ever been to a Red Dogs game before?" Leila asked. "Big Dog is a cartoon mascot that walks around, giving high fives and throwing t-shirts. Also, he judges the hot dog race."

"OK, there's no such thing as a hot dog race at a baseball game."

"No, it's this thing they do at Red Dogs games now where three hot dog mascots race around the bases. It's the best part of the game. The last time I was here, Big Dog took the onion hot dog's hand and got down on one knee like he was asking her to marry him. He's really funny."

"Well he'd better get here quick because Baxter is about to lose it," Kait said.

Leila nodded. Now that she thought about it, it was kind of amazing that all these dogs were behaving so well despite being packed so close together. While they waited for Big Dog, Leila kept herself busy by trying to identify all the different breeds of dogs in the hallway. A kid she recognized from school was petting a fluffy, yellow dog. Golden retriever. Easy. Next to him was a dog big enough to ride on. Leila guessed that one was a Great Dane. Across from the Great Dane, a teenage girl held a purse with a little, pointy-eared dog sticking out of it. Definitely a chihuahua. Then next to the teenager...

Leila elbowed Kait. "Hey!"

"What?"

"Isn't that Jenny Jones from Mrs. Liggins's class? What's she doing here?"

Kait took a break from comforting Baxter to look up. "Yeah, that's Jenny. She's probably walking in the parade. What's wrong with that?"

"Nothing, except she always talks about how much she hates dogs, right? Doesn't she only like cats or something?

Plus, she's not even holding a leash—she only has that bookbag."

"She's probably just got a little dog in there or..." Kait got distracted halfway through her answer by Baxter trying to squirm out of her arms. "Hey, come on!"

Suit Lady got everyone's attention again. This time, she had to really yell since the dogs sounded much louder in the small hallway. "I'm sorry Big Dog's not here yet!" she said. "He was supposed to be waiting for us. I'm going to find him. Everyone stay put for just a minute longer."

Kait turned to Leila with a worried expression. "Wait, where is she going?! It's so hot down here! Are you hot? I feel like I can't breathe!"

"It's OK," Leila said. "Just breathe. We'll be out of here in a minute."

Kait wasn't the only one starting to

panic. Many of the dogs had begun to bark and howl. Others were pawing at each other. The Great Dane had begun sniffing Jenny Jones's bookbag suspiciously.

"I can't breathe!" Kait said, holding her throat. "It's so smelly!"

The Great Dane was now poking the bag with his snout. Jenny noticed and tried to move, but that only made the dog poke harder. Suddenly, a head popped out of the bookbag.

It was a cat.

The Great Dane's eyes got wide. The cat's eyes got wide. Every dog in the hallway turned to the intruder. For a moment, everything was silent.

Then, the place erupted.

CAT'S OUT OF THE BAG

"Are you sure you're all OK?" Leila's dad asked for the third time.

Leila nodded. Five minutes after escaping the hallway, her ears were still ringing, but at least they worked. "Yeah, Dad. It was just a little scary for a second."

"THAT WAS MORE THAN A LITTLE SCARY!" Kait shouted a bit too loudly, probably because her ears were ringing too.

Kait was right—for a few moments, nothing in the world was scarier than that hallway. As soon as the dogs realized that a cat was in their presence, they all went bonkers. The sound of 200 dogs barking at once bounced around the small hallway, which made the dogs even crazier. Several of them escaped from their owners and started a stampede. Fortunately, Jenny was standing near the end of the hallway, so she was able to escape before any of the dogs got her cat. Unfortunately, her end of the hallway happened to be the one near the field. Jenny sprinted onto the field with two dozen dogs following her, their owners chasing after the leashes. Even now, five minutes later, a few dogs were still running wild in the outfield.

Kait and Leila had joined the crowd running back to the stands. It was a tight squeeze, but they'd all made it. With all the scared people and dogs trying to get through the same door at the same time, it was a small miracle that everyone seemed to be fine. In fact, Nugget was more than fine—he looked ready to do it again.

"Well, that was an adventure," Leila's dad said. "You girls get your things together, and we'll head home."

"But, Dad! What about the Pup Parade?"

Leila's dad pointed to a guy tripping over second base as he chased a poodle through the infield. "At this point, they'll be lucky to get the game in. They're not doing the parade."

"Please, can we just wait another few minutes? At least until the hot dog race!"

"That's not until the sixth inning," Mr. Beal said. "Look, I know it's a bummer. I was looking forward to watching the game too. But..."

"Oh, look! Let's ask her!" Kait

interrupted, pointing to the suit lady from earlier. "Excuse me!" she said. The woman looked her way. She had dirt on both knees, and some of her hair was sticking straight up. "Do you know if we're still going to do the Pup Parade?"

"Yes!" the lady said. "Wait, no. I don't know, probably not. Have any of you seen Big Dog?"

"No, is he missing?" Kait asked.

"Yes! That's why all this is happening! We couldn't find Big Dog, and then the dogs just snapped."

"So if we find Big Dog, we can do the parade?" Leila asked hopefully.

The lady looked over Leila's shoulders and pointed. "There he is!"

Leila turned around, expecting to see a giant, red dog. Instead, it was a skinny college kid with worried eyes. "Mrs. Gilmore!" he said.

"Nick! What happened? Where's the costume?!"

"Mrs. Gilmore, I'm so sorry. I can't find it anywhere!"

"What do you mean you can't find it? I handed it to you this morning."

"I know! And then I hung it up in the mascot closet. When I came back, it was gone!"

"Are you sure you didn't forget where you put it?"

"Yeah! It's not an easy thing to misplace."

"Nick! You know how important that costume is! If you didn't misplace it, then what happened?"

"Mrs. Gilmore," Nick looked around and leaned in. "I think someone stole it!"

"Who would..."

"We're on the case!" Kait shouted.

PUPPY PALS

Both Nick and Mrs. Gilmore whipped their heads around. They didn't realize the girls had been listening the whole time.

"The what?" Mrs. Gilmore asked.

"The case!" Kait said. "We're on the case! Leila here is a professional detective, and my name is Kait. I'm her sidekick."

"That's very nice, girls. But I don't think you can help."

"You ever heard of the Englewood Elementary treasure?" Kait asked. "Leila's the one who found it. No big deal."

"Uh, no, I haven't heard of that,"

Mrs. Gilmore said.

"That was you?!" Nick asked. "I saw that on the news! That's so cool!"

Leila blushed. "I had a lot of help."

Mrs. Gilmore's radio crackled. "Stacey, can you get us some help on the field? This dog's too fast!"

"I'll do that now," she said into the walkie-talkie. Then she looked at Nick. "I need you to find that costume. It's expensive, and Mr. Gilmore has had it for a long time."

"I understand," Nick said.

"Now if these girls think they can help, take them with you."

"Oh, no," Nick said. "That won't be necessary."

The radio crackled again. "Two more dogs just jumped onto the field! What do we do?!"

"Coming!" Mrs. Gilmore said into the

18

radio. She turned back to Nick. "Looks like I'm going to be running around all day. If they can't help find the costume, at least they can watch the puppies." Then she walked away before Nick could protest.

Puppies?! The girls turned to Leila's dad. "Pleeeeaaaase?!"

"You still have the emergency phone Mom gave you, right?" he asked Leila.

"Of course!" Leila dug the flip phone out of her pocket.

"OK. But stay with an adult."

"Hooray!" Kait spun around with Baxter. He was not amused.

"Come with me," Nick grumbled.

The girls followed Nick back underneath the stadium and turned into a small room off the main hallway. When Nick opened the door, a blast of air conditioning hit the girls.

"Brrr!" Kait wrapped her arms around her body. "Are you guys using this room as a freezer? Why... AWWWWWWW!"

Kait forgot all about the temperature when she spotted a blanket in the corner of the room bundling a litter of the cutest puppies ever. "They're adorable!" Kait said. "What kind are they?"

"I don't know," Nick replied. "They're Mrs. Gilmore's. I think they're Labs or something."

Nugget bounded to the puppies and started sniffing and licking like crazy.

"Can I hold one of them?" Kait asked.

"Sure. You two keep an eye on these guys while I try to find the costume," Nick said, walking out the door.

"Eeee!" Kait squealed as she ran toward the puppies.

"Wait!" Leila grabbed her shoulder. "We're here to solve a mystery, remember?"

Kait rolled her eyes. Nick did too. "Look," he said. "It's very nice of you to offer, but this is my problem. I've got this."

Leila stood her ground. "Since the parade got canceled because of this, it's our problem too. If we find the costume before the end of the game, maybe we can save the parade." She took out her notebook. "Can you tell us everything you know about the missing costume? Has this ever happened before?"

Nick sighed. The girls didn't look like they were going anywhere. "Fine. I don't know if the costume has ever been stolen before because this is the first time I've ever been Big Dog. Mrs. Gilmore's husband usually does it. He's been Big Dog for almost 20 years."

"Why are you doing it today?"

"He just had knee surgery," Nick said. "That's why the puppies are here too. He can't take care of them by himself at home, so Mrs. Gilmore's watching them here. Anyways, my mom is friends with Mrs. Gilmore, and she volunteered me to be Big Dog for the summer. Looks like I lost the job after one day."

"So how long was the costume out of your sight?"

"Not long. Maybe 15 minutes. I hung it up over there when I left the room around 11," Nick pointed to a coat rack with an empty hanger. "And when I came back, it was gone."

Leila wrote that down in her notebook, then looked around for clues. The room was pretty empty—there was the coat rack, a tall mirror, a coffee pot, a refrigerator, a few chairs and...

Leila picked up a wallet from one of the chairs. "Is this yours?" she asked.

Nick's eyes got big. "I can't believe I left that out!"

This wasn't adding up. A thief walked past a wallet lying out in the open? Leila looked back at the puppies. There were four of them. "Are any puppies missing?"

Nick shrugged. "I can't remember how many there were."

"Oh, I have an idea!" Kait piped up. "We can check the security cameras!"

"I don't think they have any in here," Nick said.

"Can we check? Oh, please, please, please?!" Kait loved spying on people, so a room full of camera screens was a dream come true for her.

"I saw a room that said 'Security' down the hall," Leila offered.

"We can't just leave the puppies," Nick said.

Leila looked back. Nugget and Baxter had curled up next to their new friends. Baxter was already asleep, and Nugget was still licking their blanket.

"Nugget!" Leila said.

He looked up with his tongue half-sticking out of his mouth.

"Stop it!"

He stuck his tongue back in and laid his head on top of one of the puppies.

"Our dogs will keep them safe," Kait said. "Now let's go!"

Kait led the way to the security room.

One wall of the room had six TV screens, all with 16 different camera feeds going at once. "This is great!" Kait said. "Let's try to find Leila's dad!"

"Kait!" Leila complained. "Focus!"

"Right," Kait sat and started scanning screens. "What are we looking for?"

"Anything suspicious," Leila said.

"OK!" Kait edged closer to the screens and squinted. "That guy looks a little too excited to be at a baseball game. Baseball is boring. And she's typing something on her phone. Can we zoom in to see what she's typing? Oh, that guy is dressed up just like one of the players! That's weird!"

"He is one of the players," Nick said.

"OK. Less weird. WHOA!"

"What is it?" Leila asked.

"Big Dog! I saw him!"

"Where?!"

"Over there!" Kait pointed to a screen showing dozens of people walking by a row of concession stands.

"Are you sure you saw the costume?" Nick asked.

"Of course! Yeah, I'm pretty sure. I mean, probably."

Leila and Nick gave each other skeptical looks.

"How do you rewind?" Kait asked.

"I don't know!" Nick said. "This is my first day on the job! I don't think we're even allowed in here!"

Nick got up to leave, but Leila grabbed his arm. "There!" she said. "We need to go there!"

She pointed to a screen showing another small room underneath the stadium. Sitting in a chair in the middle of the room was Jenny Jones, the girl who'd started the stampede.

CATS RULE

"Jenny? You think it was Jenny?!" Kait asked as they hurried down the hall.

"Keep your voice down," Leila said. "I don't know, but it kind of makes sense."

"You'll have to explain that to me before we accuse this girl," Nick said.

"Whoever stole the costume passed up your wallet," Leila said. "So they probably weren't interested in the money they could make by selling the costume, right?"

"I guess."

"Then what did they want? There aren't many things you can do with a six-foot-tall mascot costume. What if they were trying to ruin Bark at the Park?"

"I don't get it," Nick said.

But Kait did. "Oh wow! Jenny loves making dogs look dumb!"

Leila nodded. "What if she hid the costume so we couldn't start the parade, then she brought out her cat when all the dogs were squished together to make them go crazy?"

"Whoaaaaaaaaa," Kait said. "What an evil supervillain plan! She's basically the Joker!"

Nick wasn't buying it. "OK, maybe she's the Joker, or maybe—just maybe—she's a scared kid who thought it was pet day at the ballpark instead of just dog day. What do you think is more likely?"

When he put it that way, Leila thought that maybe her idea sounded a bit silly. But before she could answer,

Kait piped up. "Joker. Definitely the Joker." She looked through the window in the door to her left and saw Jenny holding her cat. "This it?" she asked.

Nick nodded as he opened the door. "Just let me do the talking, OK?" he said.

"Mom!" Jenny yelled when she saw the door begin to open. "I was so scared! I..." she stopped when she saw Leila, Kait and Nick instead of her mom.

"Scared of what?" Kait asked. "Scared someone would figure out your evil plan? Well, guess what? We already did!"

"Evil plan?! What are you talking about? Where's my mom?"

"Your mom can't save you now!" Kait said with her finger in the air.

Nick grabbed Kait's finger and shoved it down. "I'm so sorry," he said to Jenny. "This was such a bad idea. We were just going."

"Wait," Leila said. "Hey, Jenny. Sorry about all this. Big Dog's missing, and we're just trying to help Nick find it. Do you think you could help us?"

Jenny held her cat closer. "Why would I help you find a big dog? Fifi almost got killed by a big dog earlier!"

"That must have been so scary for you," Leila said.

"It was! I knew Fifi was scared in that tunnel full of dogs, but she was being so brave and quiet, and that dumb dog decided to go after her anyways."

"Oh, don't you blame this on the dogs!" Kait yelled. "You were the one..."

Leila elbowed Kait. "What made you bring Fifi into that tunnel in the first place?" she asked.

Jenny put her nose in the air. "Cuz cats are better than dogs."

"Excuse me?" Kait said, squinting and leaning in close.

"You heard me." Jenny squinted back. "Cats. Are. Better. And even though everyone knows they're better, cats aren't allowed at the baseball game. Ever!" She looked at Nick. "Why is there no Meow at the Park? Huh? Why not?"

Nick put up his hands. "Don't look at me! This is my first day!"

"Just because you like cats doesn't mean you have to ruin dog day for everyone else," Kait said.

"Ruin it? I was just trying to show that cats could do Bark at the Park too! Even better than dogs!"

"You really should have left the cat at home," Nick said. "That was dangerous."

"Yeah," Jenny shot back. "You know why? Cuz dogs are dumb."

Leila was just about to give up when she noticed Jenny's bookbag. Even though she'd taken the cat out of it, it still looked full. "I'm glad that you and your cat are safe," Leila said. "Last thing so we can go—can you open your bookbag real quick?"

"What?" Jenny asked. "No. Why do you need to see inside my bookbag?"

Kait noticed how big the bookbag was too and gasped. "Cuz you've got a Big Dog costume in there!"

Jenny shook her head hard. "No way, Jose!"

"If you just open it real quick, we'll leave you alone," Leila pleaded.

"Listen, I saw some big, dumb mascot walking around earlier," Jenny said. "It was by the bleachers or something. Why don't you go check it out?"

"Just open your bookbag!" Kait said as she started unzipping the bag herself. "What are you trying to hide?!"

"Nothing!" Jenny yanked the bag back so hard that it unzipped all the way, and poster board flung across the room. The sign landed face-up on the floor so everyone could see its message—CATS RULE! DOGS DROOL!

Kait folded her arms. "Oh, but you weren't trying to ruin Bark at the Park. You just wanted to bring your little, innocent cat."

Jenny stuck her nose in the air. "I'm not saying another word until my mom gets here."

"Fine!" Kait said.

"FINE!" Jenny said.

"HA! You just said another word!"

"We're leaving," Nick said. "NOW."

Kait started whining as they walked out of the room. "We got her, though! She was trying to ruin Bark at the Park!"

"We didn't get anyone," Leila sighed. "She didn't have the costume."

"Then she must have hidden it somewhere!" Kait said as she opened the door to the mascot room. "We'll find it if it's the last thing we..."

Kait gasped. There was Baxter, standing at the door with his tail wagging. There was Nugget, still sniffing and licking. And then next to Nugget were three cute, little puppies.

One was missing.

NO DOGS ALLOWED

"Baxter! Where did the puppy go?!" Kait yelled.

Baxter heard the word, "go," and perked up. He really wanted to go.

"Oh, this is bad," Nick said. "This is really, really bad. Losing the costume is one thing. But losing a puppy? I'm dead."

"Back to the security room!" Leila said. "If we hurry, we might be able to spot it!"

Nugget raced back to the security room with Leila, Kait and Nick. Leila started scanning the video feeds as soon as she stepped inside. "Kait, take those screens! Nick, you look over there!" Leila focused on the screens showing the bleachers. So many people! She pulled Nugget up to take a look. He was great at spotting dogs.

"No kids in the security office!" an angry female voice commanded from the doorway. Leila spun around in her spinny chair to apologize. Before she could even turn all the way around, the woman noticed Nugget and gasped. "NO DOGS IN THE SECURITY OFFICE!"

"You're the one with the dog!" Kait yelled back.

When Leila finally turned all the way around, she discovered what Kait meant. The yelling voice belonged to a stern security officer holding Mrs. Gilmore's missing puppy. The woman had a nametag on her chest that said, "Franklin."

"I'm allowed to have this dog! I belong here. You know who doesn't belong here? All ya'll!"

"Oh no," Leila said. "She just meant that we were looking for that puppy, and we're happy you found it!"

"Found it? It was never lost!"

"Oh, because we didn't see it..."

"I fed it, if that's what you mean.

They told me some kid named Rick was supposed to take care of these dogs."

"You mean Nick?" Nick asked, sheepishly raising his hand.

"You Nick?" Officer Franklin asked.

Nick nodded.

She handed him the puppy. "They've got me feeding puppies, watching kids, chasing dogs. They don't pay me enough for this."

"I'm sorry, ma'am," Leila said. "I was supposed to watch the puppies with my friend, Kait, while Nick looked for a mascot costume that may have been stolen. Have you seen it?"

"The dog one?"

"That's right."

"No," Officer Franklin said. "It's usually hanging up in the mascot room next to my uniform. It wasn't there today. When did it go missing?"

Leila looked at her notebook. "He walked out of the room for 15 minutes around—what time did you say, Nick? Like 11 a.m.?"

Nick suddenly looked uncomfortable. "I don't know. It's hard to remember."

"Yeah, it was 11," Officer Franklin said. "You were leaving just as I was getting here. Remember?"

"Ohhhhhhh, uh, yeah, I guess," Nick said.

"Well all the costumes were gone by then," Officer Franklin said.

Leila looked up from her notebook. "What?"

"My uniform was the only thing on the rack when I got here. He must have misremembered."

"Do you think we could look at the tape from the security camera?" Leila asked.

"There aren't any cameras in that room," Officer Franklin said. "People get dressed in there."

"OK, well maybe we could look at the video from the hallway to see who else might have gone in that room?"

Officer Franklin's radio squawked. "Can we get security to section 106? A loose beagle won't leave the hot dog guy alone."

Officer Franklin huffed. "One thing after another. Listen, I can try to help you later, OK?" She shook her head as she left the office. Then she yelled back, "I meant what I said earlier! You kids get out of my office!"

Leila, Kait and Nick hurried back to the mascot room. Once inside, Nugget licked the puppies again. He was happy to see his new friends. Leila closed the door and turned to Nick with her arms folded across her chest. "OK. Spill it."

"Spill what?" Nick asked.

"You know what!" Kait said, even though she clearly didn't know herself.

"Why did you fib about when the costume went missing?" Leila asked.

"I didn't fib! I misremembered!" Nick said, even though he was making a guilty face.

Kait lit up. She'd been waiting to interrogate someone all day. "Spill it, pal! Or I'll sic my vicious dog on you!" She pointed at Baxter, who was trying to curl up and get comfy. Baxter sighed.

Nick looked around the room. "I'll tell you guys, but you have to promise not to tell Mrs. Gilmore."

JUICY RED

"How about we call Mrs. Gilmore right this second?" Kait said.

"And tell her what? I didn't steal anything!" Nick insisted.

Kait pointed to Leila, who pulled the emergency phone out of her pocket. Kait grabbed the phone and started punching in a random number. "Hope she believes that because we've got two witnesses in this room who heard you confess. Actually, eight if you count the dogs."

Nick looked nervous again. "Put that away!" he said. "I told you, I didn't steal the costume! But..." he looked around again and lowered his voice. "I wasn't completely honest."

Kait hovered her finger above the send button and looked at Nick with her eyebrows raised in a "tell me more" kind of way.

Nick sighed. "Mrs. Gilmore has spent the last week reminding me over and over how much that costume means to her husband. She has a bunch of rules for wearing it – rules that would be impossible for anyone to follow."

"Like what?" Leila asked.

"Like no sweating in the costume, even though it's basically a head-to-toe coat you're wearing in the middle of the summer. I mean, it's made of fleece. Fleece!"

"How did she expect you not to sweat?"

"I was supposed to come back to this

room and cool down every time I got hot throughout the game. That's why they keep the air conditioning blasting so cold. But even then, I'm gonna sweat. It'd be impossible not to!"

"OK, that is kind of crazy," Kait admitted. "What other rules did she have?"

"No running in the costume, no dancing on top of the dugout, check all hands for nacho cheese before giving high fives. But the craziest one is no drinking pop while wearing the costume."

"Why is that so crazy?" Leila asked.

Nick motioned to the refrigerator in the corner. "Being a mascot is hard work, so the Red Dogs keep a refrigerator stocked with all sorts of drinks."

Kait opened the fridge. "Whoa! They have everything in here! Fancy bottled

water, Gatorade, iced tea. Wait, is that..."
She dug into the back of the fridge.
"JUICY RED!"

"Exactly," Nick said. "And that's why
the 'no drinking in the costume' rule is
the most impossible."

"I don't get it," Leila said, examining
the Juicy Red can.

"You'd understand if you tasted it!"
Kait said.

Leila opened the pop and took a sip.
It was super-duper sweet. Like if

someone figured out how to turn cotton candy into a fizzy drink. "Pretty good."

"Pretty good? Pretty good?!" Kait asked with wide eyes. "It's the best thing ever! And you can't buy it anywhere! They stopped making it like two years ago!" She turned to Nick. "How did you get this?!"

"I guess Mr. Gilmore loves it, so the Red Dogs bought him a huge supply before the company went out of business. Anyways, I noticed the Juicy Red this morning after I'd already put on the costume. I couldn't believe it—Juicy Red is my favorite drink of all time! Obviously, I had to take a sip."

"Obviously," Kait agreed.

"As soon as I started drinking, one of the puppies tugged on my leg. I knew I wasn't supposed to be drinking, so that little tug startled me so much that I spilled Juicy Red all over the inside of the costume."

Leila looked back down at the pop. It was almost neon red. "That must be Mrs. Gilmore's worst nightmare."

"Exactly," Nick said. "As soon as it happened, I turned the costume inside out and tried to wash it with the bottled water. When that didn't work, I ran to the laundry room where they clean the players' uniforms to see if they had anything for the stain. So instead of hanging it back in the closet, I draped it inside out over that chair to let it dry. When I came back, it was gone!"

"And you don't have any idea who might have taken it?"

"For a while, I figured it was that security lady trying to get me in trouble with Mrs. Gilmore. But she hasn't said anything yet, so it's probably not her."

Nick leaned in closer. "I think someone's using it for blackmail."

"That makes sense," Kait said. "Wait, what's blackmail?"

"When someone knows a secret you're trying to keep, they can threaten to tell everyone to make you pay money," Nick said.

"Oh, well I know how we can fix this," Leila said.

"How?"

"We just tell Mrs. Gilmore what happened."

"What?!" Nick yelled. "No! Didn't you hear anything I just said! That's exactly what we don't need to do!"

"But if she knows, then the blackmail won't work. Plus, the pop will come out in the wash. Mrs. Gilmore might be mad for a little bit, but she'll understand."

"Nope, nope, nope. No way."

At that moment, the door opened, and a head popped in. "It's the fourth inning, and all the dogs are under control," Mrs. Gilmore said. "Please tell me you found my husband's costume."

SUPER-DUPER FIRED

"Go home. You're fired."

"But, Mrs. Gilmore..." Nick protested.

"You're fired," Mrs. Gilmore repeated. Her arms were folded. After she'd walked into the room, Leila, Kait and Nick had danced around the truth for awhile before Kait finally spilled it. "How could you not be fired?!" Mrs. Gilmore asked. "You ruined my husband's costume and then lost it before you even started your first day!"

"I'm sorry. I shouldn't have drunk pop while wearing the costume."

"My husband loves Juicy Red! LOVES it! And in 20 years, he's never drunk it in the costume! You know why? Because he takes care of his stuff!"

Leila stepped up. "Mrs. Gilmore, I know you're upset."

"I'm furious!"

"But the thief probably won't leave the stadium until the game's over, right?"

"Hmf."

"So maybe you could unfire Nick for a little bit so he can help find the costume before it gets away for good."

Mrs. Gilmore thought about it for a second. "You are temporarily unfired," she finally said. "But after this game, you're super-duper fired. Understood?"

"Yes, ma'am."

Without another word, Mrs. Gilmore stomped out and slammed the door.

Nick turned to the girls. "You happy now? I knew that would happen!"

"Maybe we can still get your job back," Leila said.

"How?!"

"You figure out how to get Juicy Red out of clothes. We'll search the stadium for the costume thief."

"You're never going to find it," Nick said with his head in his hands. "The stadium's too big."

Leila and Kait clipped their leashes onto their dogs. "Don't worry," Leila said. "We're going to recruit some help." She scooped up one of the puppies and smiled. "Everyone loves a puppy!"

Kait grinned and picked one up too. "Puppies are the best!"

Leila gave Nick the number to the emergency phone in case he found anything and marched back out of the tunnel with Kait. The girls blinked a couple times when the sunlight hit their faces. "I actually kind of don't get it," Kait said. "What are we doing with the puppies?"

"Follow my lead," Leila said as she fitted Nugget's Red Dogs hat onto the puppy.

Just then, the girls heard an "awwwwwwwww" to their left. They turned to see the chihuahua owner from the tunnel. She was pointing to the puppies. "They're sooooo cute!" She elbowed her friend with an Australian Shepherd. "Look!" She turned to Leila and Kait. "Can we pet them?"

"Of course!" Leila said. Soon, several more dog owners had gathered around. When the crowd got big enough, Leila told them about Big Dog. "Have any of you seen anything suspicious?" she asked.

"It's that Clifford dog, right?" Chihuahua girl turned to her friend. "Didn't we see him earlier?"

Her friend shrugged. "Maybe by home plate?"

Leila and Kait thanked the group then started walking toward home plate. They got ten steps before...

"AWWWWW!"

Another large group gathered around the girls. This group hadn't seen anything, but they all agreed to keep an eye out. One of the boys had a German Shepherd who'd been trained to find things with his nose. Give the dog a sniff of Juicy Red, and he'd find the costume in no time, the boy promised. Ten seconds after they left the German Shepherd, the girls got stopped again. This time, they met a girl cavapoo named Penelope that looked just like Nugget. Nugget immediately fell in love. The two dogs started playing and got their leashes hopelessly tangled in seconds. Penelope's owner promised to walk her dog all the way around the stadium to look for Big Dog.

By the sixth inning, Leila had snapped 20 pictures of Nugget with his new doggy friends, Kait had to borrow treats from 12 different people to keep Baxter moving and half the stadium had volunteered to search for Big Dog.

"Nobody knows anything, and Baxter might explode if he eats one more treat," Kait finally said. "Do you have any other ideas?"

"The costume was underneath the stadium, so the person who took it probably works for the team," Leila said. "Asking the fans is good because it gives us more eyes to help look, but if we're going to find the costume, we're going to have to go places most fans can't."

"How are we going to do that?" Kait asked.

Leila smiled and walked to the "Krazy Kettle Korn" concession stand. "Excuse me," she said. "Do you happen to have a water bowl for my puppy?"

The woman at the counter smiled at the puppy. "Oooo, you thirsty? You a thirsty puppy?" Then she looked back up at Leila. "No problem, come back here!" Inside the concession stand, the woman gave the puppies some water and Nugget and Baxter some popcorn. While she did, Leila and Kait took a quick look around. Nothing suspicious. The girls tried the same thing at Nacho Heaven with the same results.

When they got to Big Dog's Chili Dogs, Leila got a text. "Do you have any vinegar?" she asked the cashier after looking at her phone.

"We do if you buy fries."

"Oh. Hey, look at my puppy!"

The cashier put her hand over her mouth. "Oh my gosh, that is the cutest puppy I've ever seen!"

After every worker at Big Dog's Chili

Dogs petted the puppy, Leila got her free vinegar after all.

"Why do you need that?" Kait asked.

Leila shrugged and pointed to the press box. "Let's look in there." When the two girls and four dogs marched into the press box, the reporters all looked alarmed. They looked even more alarmed when Leila asked her question. "Do any of you have newspaper for my puppies? I think they have to go to the bathroom."

While the reporters all scrambled to find paper, Kait snooped in every drawer and cubby hole for any sign of a costume. Nothing. The girls didn't give up. After the press box, they found ways to get into the video booth, the scoreboard operator's room and the umpire lounge. Still nothing.

Leila sighed as she plopped onto a bench. "That's it. I'm all out of ideas. I thought for sure we'd find something."

"Don't feel bad," Kait said. "You did your best. Do you want to break the news to Nick, or should I?"

"We can in a second. I want to rest first." Leila pulled out her phone and started scrolling through pictures. There were some really cute dogs. She especially liked the beagle and the one that looked like a fox and Nugget's girlfriend... "Whoa!" Leila said when she got to Penelope's picture. "Look at this!"

Kait squinted at the picture. "What? I don't see anything. Can you make it bigger?" She touched the screen and tried to stretch out the picture.

"That doesn't work on a flip phone," Leila said. "But look up there in the corner. What does that look like?"

Kait squinted some more, then she gasped. "Is that Big Dog?!"

MUSH

With new energy, Leila and Kait sprang off the bench and restarted their search for Big Dog. The thief wasn't hiding the costume—he was walking around in plain sight! It didn't take the girls long to find their target. "There!" Kait screeched.

Leila followed her finger across the stadium. "Where?"

"There! Next to the bleachers! I saw a big dog snout for a second, and then it disappeared into the crowd!"

"Let's go!" Leila and Kait bounded toward the left field bleachers.

Unfortunately, the puppies that had helped them make so much progress just a few minutes before were now slowing them down. When they finally got to the left field bleachers, Big Dog was nowhere to be found. "Has anyone seen the mascot?!" Kait yelled.

"Over there," someone pointed.

Leila looked up to see a big, floppy ear near the third-base dugout. "He's headed underground!" she said. The girls raced toward the tunnel as best they could through the crowd. "Excuse me," Leila said as she tried to politely push through. "Oh, sorry. Sorry, ma'am. Excuse me, sir. Can we just squeeze through here? Nugget, we don't have time for that!"

With Big Dog getting away, Kait pulled out one last trick. "Baxter! Mush!"

Baxter, who to this point had been half-heartedly waddling through the stadium, broke into a full gallop. Nugget's eyes lit up when he saw Baxter sprint ahead and joined him. Side-by-side, they looked like two tiny sled dogs. The crowd noticed and quickly parted to avoid getting bulldozed by the furry bullets.

"What did you do?!" Leila gasped as she struggled to catch up.

"It's a trick I taught him when I was little," Kait said, concentrating on holding the puppy under her arm like a football. "I thought he could pull me around on a sled."

The girls were closing in on their target. They just had one more corner to round. "Clear the way, everyone!" Kait yelled. "We're saving Big—OOOF!"

Someone stepped in her way just as she turned the corner. It was Jenny. Kait dropped the leash and almost dropped the puppy as she fell down.

"WHAT ARE YOU DOING?!" Kait yelled as she scrambled for the leash. "You're letting him get away!"

"Sorry, but you're wrong," Jenny said.

Before she could question Jenny, Leila caught a glimpse of the tunnel door closing. A mascot tail disappeared inside. "Quick!" she yelled as she let go of

Nugget's leash. "Before the door locks!" Nugget darted around fans, scampered between a hot dog vendor's legs and leaped over a small Yorkie in the aisle. He squeezed through the doorway just in time, and his leash even got stuck in the crack to keep the door from closing all the way.

"Let's go!" Leila yelled.

Kait picked herself up and got Baxter. "You're not gonna get away with this!" she shouted back to Jenny.

"I'm not getting away with anything! You're..."

The girls disappeared into the tunnel before Jenny could finish her sentence. "There!" Leila said, pointing to a tall figure disappearing around the corner. She rescued Nugget and took off again. By this time, Baxter was pooped, so Kait scooped him underneath her other arm.

Carrying the two dogs, Kait was having a hard time walking, let alone jogging.

Nick stuck his head out of the mascot room when he heard the commotion. "What's going on?"

"We (gasp) found (gasp) Big Dog," Kait panted. "Take these." Kait and Leila dumped Baxter and the puppies at Nick's feet.

"Where?" he asked. "Down here?! I haven't seen him!"

Before Nick could get his answer, the girls and Nugget ran off again. The girls rounded the corner, then gasped. In the dim light, they could make out the silhouettes of not one, not two, but THREE Big Dogs jogging together at the end of the hallway! What?! Were they dealing with a gang of mascot thieves?!

Nugget led the girls in one final sprint to catch up before the Big Dogs rounded the third corner. But just as they started gaining ground, a head poked out of the security room. "No running through the halls!" Officer Franklin yelled.

The girls slowed to the fastest a person could shuffle without technically running. "We found Big Dog!" Leila said on her way by the security officer. "Actually we found three of them!"

Officer Franklin wrinkled her nose in disgust. "Three Big Dogs?! You girls need to stop this nonsense right now!"

"No can do!" Kait shouted as she shuffled faster. She turned to Leila. "Jenny and the police lady are both in on this too? How big is this gang?!" From up around the corner, the girls heard a big door open. Sunlight streamed into the hallway.

"Quick!" Leila shouted. "They're escaping!"

The girls skidded around the corner

and flew out the open door to find...

...Three giant hot dogs sprinting ahead.

Those weren't Big Dogs—they were big hot dogs, dressed up with dog tails, snouts and floppy ears to celebrate Bark at the Park. This was the sixth-inning hot dog race, not an elaborate mascot heist. Wait a second. If this was the hot dog race...

Leila looked up to find herself standing in the middle of left field with 10,000 pairs of eyes staring right back at her.

STADIUM JAIL

Stadium jail.

That's what Officer Franklin insisted on calling it. She explained that some professional stadiums have real jail cells with metal bars and everything to hold unruly fans, but the Middleburg Red Dogs only had this little room that they sometimes used for stadium jail and sometimes used for lost kids like Jenny Jones. "But make no mistake," Officer Franklin said right before she slammed the door on Leila, Kait and Nugget. "Right now, it's stadium jail."

Leila was on the verge of tears. She'd

hardly ever been in trouble before, let alone gotten thrown into jail. Kait, on the other hand, was defiant. "We'll fight this," Kait said. "We'll take it to the Supreme Court if we have to! This just burns me up. We were trying to do something good, and we make one little mistake..."

"Running onto the field is a big mistake," Leila corrected.

"...We make one ITTY, BITTY mistake," Kait continued, "And suddenly we're in jail? I don't think so! Not in America!"

Leila put her head in her hands. She had gotten so swept up in the hunt for the Big Dog that she'd stopped thinking. Why would there be three Big Dog costumes? That should have made her stop right there. And the sixth inning hot dog race was always her favorite part of the game. Hadn't she just been telling Kait about it?

After three unsuccessful laps around the room trying to find something to eat, Nugget jumped into Leila's lap and curled up. As Leila petted Nugget, she got her nerve back. "The only way we're escaping this without getting grounded for life is by solving the case. So let's look back at everything we know and try to figure it out."

"OK, let's start at the beginning," Kait said. "The first thing we know is that Jenny Jones is the worst."

"No! That's not something we know! All we know is that she brought a cat and a sign to a baseball game."

"And that she tackled me and tried to stop us from finding Big Dog," Kait said.

"Actually she was trying to keep us from getting thrown into stadium jail."

Kait rolled her eyes.

"And that's not even the beginning," Leila said. "The beginning is when Mrs. Gilmore gave Nick the costume."

"Do you think Mrs. Gilmore stole her own costume so she could fire Nick?" Kait asked. "She doesn't seem to like him very much."

"She liked him just fine until he ruined the costume," Leila said. "I don't think she stole it."

"Well then maybe Nick?"

"Maybe, but I don't know why. Wouldn't he want to wait until after the game to steal the costume?"

Kait spun her chair around and sat in it backward because that seemed like something a police detective would do. "I'll tell you who I think it was," Kait said. "I think it was the security lady."

Leila thought about it for a second.

She was the only one in the room when the costume went missing. "Maybe," she finally said. "But why?"

"Because we were trying to solve a crime, and that's her job! This is what she wanted all along. She was scared because we're so much better than her at her job."

"You're saying she knew we were coming to the game, so she figured out a way to lock us up so we wouldn't take her job one day?"

"The perfect crime," Kait said, looking off into the distance like she'd just solved the biggest case of her life.

Leila shook her head. "We're missing something."

Just then the door opened. Nick walked in with Baxter and Mrs. Gilmore. "You two waiting for your parents?" Nick asked.

"Stadium jail," Kait replied matter-of-factly.

"There's no such thing as 'stadium jail,'" Mrs. Gilmore replied with squinty eyes.

"But that lady said..." Kait stopped when she saw Officer Franklin walk through the door with Leila's dad.

"You told them they were in stadium jail?" Mrs. Gilmore asked Officer Franklin.

"That's right," she said. "And I brought the judge."

Leila's dad shook his head. "Leila, how could you..."

"I'm so sorry, Dad! The hot dog was dressed up like a real dog!"

Mr. Beal looked more confused than ever. "You'll have to explain in the car. Let's go."

Leila hung her head. She really wasn't going to solve this case. "OK."

Nick stepped up. "I'm sorry about all this," he said to Leila. "I really appreciate you trying to help me, even though you're gonna get in trouble for it."

"And I'm sorry about not solving your mystery," Leila said. "I tried my best." Nugget looked sad about not finding Big

Dog too.

Nick petted Nugget. "It's OK," he said. "You guys did great." He handed Baxter over to Kait. "Your dog really liked hanging out with the puppies. He couldn't stop licking them!"

Leila's head snapped up. "What did you say?"

"It was really funny," Nick said. "He kept licking and licking."

"But Baxter doesn't like other dogs. Especially puppies."

Nick shrugged. "Well, he liked these ones. He liked them so much that he was even licking their blanket!"

Leila's eyes got wide. "I solved it!" she said.

Officer Franklin rolled her eyes. "Not again."

"No, for real! I solved it, I solved it, I solved it!"

"Solved what?" Mrs. Gilmore asked. "You know who took the costume?"

Leila nodded and pointed at Officer Franklin. "Her!"

DOG OF THE YEAR

"WHAT?!" Officer Franklin bellowed. Mrs. Gilmore looked up in surprise. Officer Franklin started walking toward Leila with her finger pointed at Leila's chest. "YOUNG LADY, YOU'D BETTER..."

"Wait, no no no. It's not bad! You didn't do it on purpose!"

"WHAT DO YOU MEAN I DIDN'T DO IT ON PURPOSE?! I'M THE SECURITY OFFICER! I THINK I'D KNOW IF I WERE STEALING SOMETHING! I WISH WE DID HAVE A STADIUM JAIL BECAUSE I

WOULD..."

"Can I just show you what I mean," Leila suggested. "I think it would be a lot easier if I showed you all."

Mrs. Gilmore sighed. "As long as it's not on the field."

Leila nodded and led the way back to the mascot room. As she did, she started her explanation. "I thought it was weird earlier that Nugget was licking the puppies so much. He loves other dogs, but he usually plays with them, not licks them."

As if to prove Leila's point, Nugget tried climbing onto Baxter's back as the two dogs walked down the hallway. Baxter stopped and grumbled.

Leila pointed to the two dogs and continued. "As weird as it was for Nugget to lick the puppies, it was downright crazy for Baxter to do that. He hates other dogs."

Kait jumped in. "He doesn't hate them, but he does like his Baxter time."

"You still haven't explained your brilliant idea of why dogs licking other dogs means I stole a costume," Officer Franklin said.

Just then, the group walked into the mascot room. Leila stopped. "It's pretty cold in here."

"It has to be," Mrs. Gilmore said. "There's no sweating in the Big Dog costume."

"That's true, but it's probably too cold for puppies."

"Way too cold for puppies!" Officer Franklin said. "You have to realize they don't wear clothes like you. And they're not big balls of fur yet like these dogs."

Nugget and Baxter looked at each other.

"So you helped, right officer?" Leila said.

"Of course I helped! I wrapped the puppies in a blanket because Rick over here forgot," she said, gesturing to Nick.

"And where did you find the blanket?"

"I don't know, it was lying somewhere in the room."

Leila smiled and started moving the puppies off their blanket. "It was draped over the chair," she said. With that, she flung open the blanket. Everyone in the room gasped. Scrunched up in a ball, it looked like a nice, soft puppy blanket. But spread out like this, everyone could see the "blanket" actually had two arms and two legs. It could only be one thing.

"BIG DOG!" Kait exclaimed.

Officer Franklin's eyes got wide. "I had no idea," she said.

"It's OK!" Leila said. "You were just trying to help! And it's white and furry inside, just like a blanket."

"Except for the big, red stain in the middle," Mrs. Gilmore said.

"Thank goodness for that stain!" Leila said. "That's what solved the case. See, Nugget doesn't usually lick other dogs, but he does love sweets."

"Like Juicy Red!" Kait exclaimed.

Leila nodded. "With the dogs licking both the puppies and the blanket, I knew something had to be up. That's when I remembered the Juicy Red."

Mrs. Gilmore picked up the costume and slowly shook her head with a smile on her face. "You girls did it! My husband's going to be so happy! What can I do to repay you? We can give you season tickets!"

Leila looked at Kait, who was making

a throw-up face at the thought of having to go to a whole season's worth of baseball games. Then Leila looked back at Mrs. Gilmore. "Actually, we thought maybe you could do something for someone else." She nodded at Nick.

"Mrs. Gilmore," Nick said. "I'm sorry for ruining your husband's costume. It's a great costume, and I should have been more careful with it. Also, um, I did find something that should take out the stain. Do you think I could try it?"

Mrs. Gilmore looked unsure. "Please, can you let him give it a try?" Leila asked. "I think it'll work." Mrs. Gilmore sighed and handed over the costume.

"Thank you!" Nick pulled baking soda out of his pocket and turned to Leila. "Did you get what I asked?"

Leila nodded and handed over the vinegar packets. Mrs. Gilmore looked nervous as Nick mixed the vinegar and baking soda together into a paste and rubbed it into the stain. Everyone gathered around. Nick looked at his phone for the next instructions. "Now, we're supposed to rinse it off and see what happens."

Nick rinsed the stain with bottled water while everyone else held their breaths. After he rinsed and wiped the stain, Mrs. Gilmore leaned in. "Whoa!" she said. "That's incredible!"

Nick could breathe again. The stain was gone. While Nick finished wiping, Mrs. Gilmore turned to Leila and Kait. "You girls truly are incredible! There must be something I can do to thank you for all you've done today!"

"Well," Leila said, looking at Nugget. "There is one more thing."

Forty-five minutes later, Nugget

happily jogged onto the field. But this time, the crowd was cheering, not gasping. After the game finished, Nugget and 200 other dogs finally got to march around the bases for the Pup Parade. Marching on Nugget's right was his new girlfriend, Penelope the cavapoo. On his left, looking happier than he'd looked all day, was Baxter. "See Baxter, this isn't so bad," Kait said, pushing the tired dog on a cart Mrs. Gilmore had dug out of a supply closet.

As she rounded first base, Leila grinned at all the familiar faces in the parade. There was the Great Dane and the Chihuahua. Mrs. Gilmore had taken a break from worrying about everything to show off her puppies. Jenny Jones had even joined the parade, proudly holding her cat. And leading everyone, practically dancing around the bases, was Nick in the Big Dog costume.

After the parade, Mrs. Gilmore stepped to a podium in front of home plate. "Every year, we crown one dog as the Middleburg Dog of the Year. Well, this year, as you might have noticed, is a little different. We wouldn't even have had Pup Parade this year if it weren't for two very special dogs. That's why—for the first time ever—we have a tie for Dog of the Year. Ladies and gentlemen, I'd like to introduce you to your Middleburg Dogs of the Year: Nugget and Baxter!"

AUTHORS' NOTE

Hope you had as much fun reading Leila and Nugget's adventure as we did writing it! If you liked this book, would you consider telling a friend or posting a short review on Amazon? We'd really appreciate the help!

Also, we'd love to hear from you! You can email us about anything at dustin@dustinbradybooks.com.

Thanks again for reading our book!

ABOUT THE AUTHORS

Deserae and Dustin Brady are the parents of Leila Brady (a baby) and Nugget Brady (a dog). They live in Cleveland, Ohio. When the hot dog mascots race each other at Cleveland Indians games, Dustin roots for Mustard, and Deserae roots for Ketchup.

ABOUT THE ILLUSTRATOR

April Brady is a professional illustrator in Pensacola, Florida. Deserae and Dustin feel lucky to have such a talented doggy-drawer as a sister-in-law.